CW00858446

LIFE ON THE ROAD

———

STEPRO

TRAVEL

BOOKS

LIFE ON THE ROAD

You need not even listen, just wait…the world will offer itself freely to you, unmasking itself. – Franz Kafka

y purchasing tickets for the observation deck, every visitor agrees that he is informed and accepts the rules which are displayed in the prominent warnings and 'Rules to be Followed', as well as the House Rules of the business building of Zagreb's skyscraper.

MURDER IS A SERIOUS CRIME

We would like that the observation deck remains a pleasant memory for all visitors.

Carelessness, recklessness or irresponsible behavior of visitors may result in unforeseeable consequences involving serious harm or death of passersby because of which a happy moment could be be turned into a tragedy for which a visitor had to spend the rest of his life in prison or working to settle the claims.

ZAGREB 360°

VIDIKOVAC I PROSTOR ZA EVENTE
U SRCU ZAGREBA

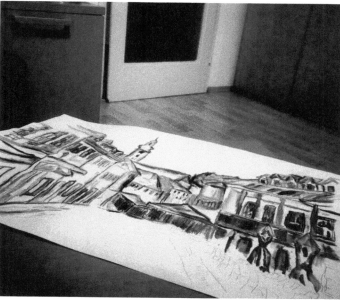

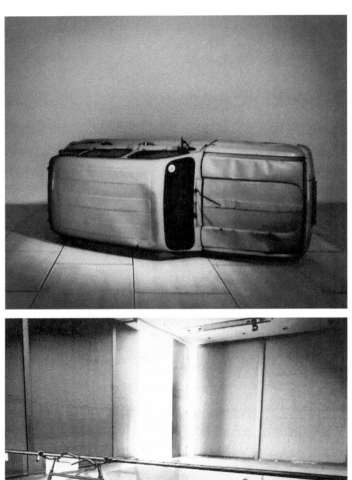

[...] something that is distancing itself [...] of leaves and branches such as the repeating [...] with, most of bearing into, and lose a something of [...] on, and do not matter. Only where its development [...] have come from the housing crash in the US, this [...] between lingers from the collapse of Yugoslavia. It's [...] so much undeveloped as it is stuck in a time that was [...] to have stopped existing. Only, it didn't. People [...] live here. Time moves on and the grass grows and dries [...] the cracks of the craggy parking lot.

[...] here is a very odd air about the place. In a city known [...] cafes there isn't a single one in sight. There is no kiosk, [...] rocery store, nor a hair salon. All of which I've come to [...] as the ubiquitous pieces of Zagreb's geography. Cafes, [...] s, hair salons, and bakeries are to Zagreb what the sand

CPSIA information can be obtained
at www.ICGtesting.com
Printed in the USA
BVHW021400220819
556528BV00023B/2582/P